GEOGRAPHY FROM A TO Z
A PICTURE GLOSSARY

GEOGRAPHY FROM A TO Z

A PICTURE GLOSSARY

By Jack Knowlton   Pictures by Harriett Barton

HarperCollins*Publishers*

Geography from A to Z: A Picture Glossary
Text copyright © 1988 by John Knowlton
Illustrations copyright © 1988 by Harriett Barton
Manufactured in Malaysia.
For information address HarperCollins Children's
Books, a division of HarperCollins Publishers,
195 Broadway, New York, NY 10007.

Library of Congress Cataloging-in-Publication Data
Knowlton, Jack.
    Geography from A to Z: a picture glossary.

    Summary: A glossary of geographic terms, from
"archipelago" to "zone," with definitions and
descriptions of the Earth's features.
    1. Geography—Dictionaries, Juvenile.   [1. Geography
—Dictionaries.]   I. Barton, Harriett.   II. Title.
G63.K63   1987   910'.3'21   86-4594
ISBN 0-690-04616-2
ISBN 0-690-04618-9 (lib. bdg.)
ISBN 0-06-446099-1 (pbk.)

Visit us on the World Wide Web!
http://www.harperchildrens.com
23 RRDA 32

For our fathers
John C. Knowlton, Sr.
and
Byron A. Wyatt

PHILIPPINE ISLANDS

Archipelago—a group of islands clustered together in an open expanse of sea or ocean. The Philippine Islands are a large archipelago.

7

Atoll—small tropical islands and reefs that encircle shallow pools of seawater called **lagoons**. Atolls and reefs are built of **coral**, the rocklike, compacted skeletons of billions upon billions of tiny sea animals called polyps.

Badland—rocky wasteland that has been carved by erosion into intricate and fantastic shapes. **Erosion** is the process by which water, wind, and ice slowly change the shape, size, and look of every feature on Earth by wearing it away.

Bay—a small area of sea or lake partly enclosed by dry land. **Coves** and **inlets** are very small bays. Some deep, sheltered bays are called **harbors**.

Beach—the sandy or rocky land at the edge of an ocean, sea, or lake. Beaches are part of the **coastline** or **seashore**.

Butte—an isolated, rocky hill or mountain with a *small* flat top. A **mesa** is similar to a butte except it has a *large* flat top.

Canyon—a deep, narrow valley with steep, rocky sides. Flowing along the bottom or **floor** of most canyons is the river that created it by carving through the surrounding rock. Small canyons are called **chasms**, **gorges**, or **ravines**.

Cape—a pointed piece of land that projects from a coastline. Small capes are often called **points** or **spits**.

Cave—a hollow underground chamber, usually one with an opening in the side of a hill or mountain. A **cavern** is a large cave or a series of connected caves.

Cliff—a sheer, steep face of rock or earth. A **bluff** is similar to a cliff but is less steep and has a broad, softly rounded face. A high, over-hanging edge of a cliff is called a **precipice**.

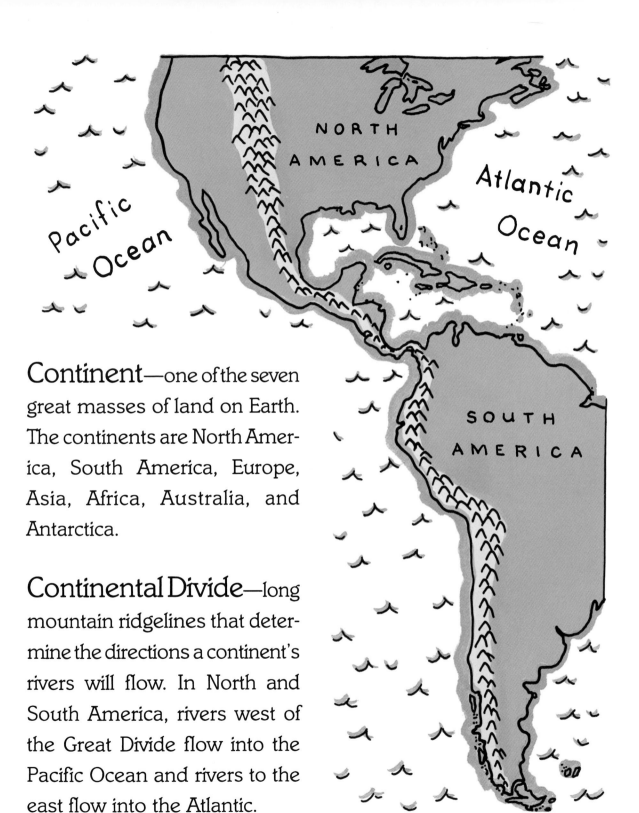

Continent—one of the seven great masses of land on Earth. The continents are North America, South America, Europe, Asia, Africa, Australia, and Antarctica.

Continental Divide—long mountain ridgelines that determine the directions a continent's rivers will flow. In North and South America, rivers west of the Great Divide flow into the Pacific Ocean and rivers to the east flow into the Atlantic.

Continental Shelf—a shallow underwater plain that is the real outer edge of a continent. The continental shelf ends at the **continental slope**, a cliff that plunges to the deep ocean floor.

Crevasse—a deep crack in either the ice on top of a glacier or the ground after an earthquake.

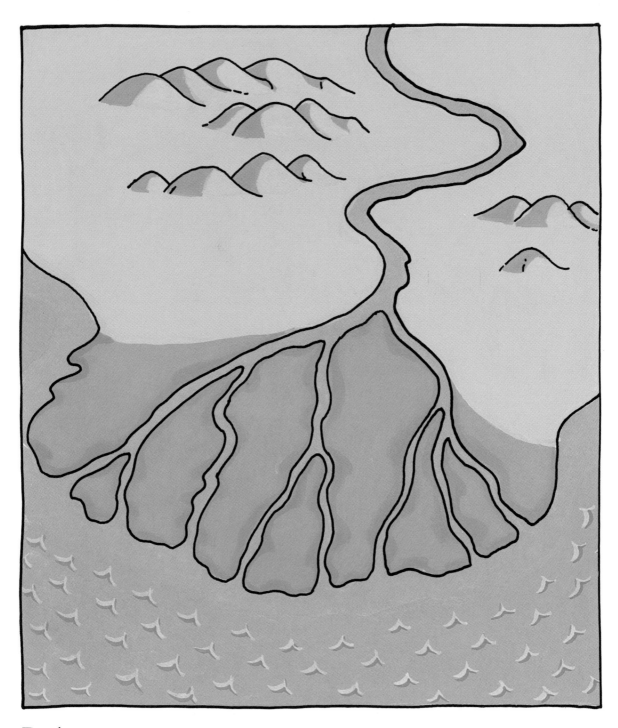

Delta—a fan-shaped deposit of mud and sand, often green with vegetation, found at the mouths of many rivers.

Desert—a very dry and desolate land that receives little or no rainfall. Most deserts are covered with rocks and stones. Only one fifth of all desert surfaces are covered with sand. An **oasis** is an isolated green spot in a desert where water flows up from an underground spring.

Dune—a mound or ridge of loose sand shaped by blowing winds. Dunes are found both in deserts and along seashores.

Fjord—a long, narrow inlet of the sea between tall, rocky cliffs.

Ford—a shallow place in a stream where people and animals can safely wade from one bank to the other.

Forest—a region thickly covered with trees and abundant under-brush. Forests are also called **woodlands** or **woods**.

Geyser—a naturally hot, or **geothermal**, spring that shoots scalding water and steam high into the air. In the Icelandic language the word *geyser* means "roaring gusher."

Glacier—a great mass of ice slowly sliding down a mountain slope or through a valley. Glaciers are very slowly moving rivers of ice.

Grassland—a vast open plain covered with natural or planted grasses. Tropical grasslands are called **savannas**. In other parts of the world grasslands have various names: **pampas**, **prairies**, **plains**, **veldts**, or **steppes**.

Gulch—a small, narrow, rocky ravine. Sometimes a violent mountain stream called a **torrent** races through a gulch. A **gully** is a jagged ditch gouged through dirt or clay by heavy rainstorms.

Gulf—a large inlet of ocean or sea that is partially surrounded by land. Gulfs are much bigger and deeper than bays.

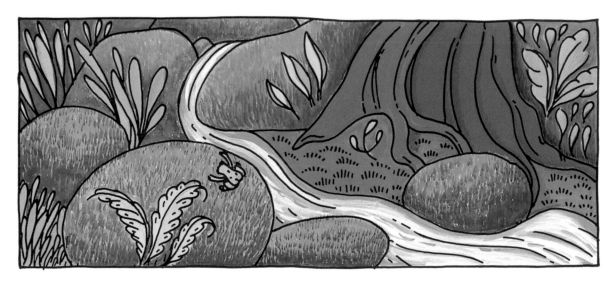

Headwater or Source—the area where a river originates and begins its journey to the sea. Headwaters are regions rich in rainfall, melting snow, and bubbling springs. **Springs** are openings in the earth where underground water flows to the surface.

Highland—a mountainous or hilly region that stands above the surrounding landscape. A **lowland** is just the opposite—a low, flat area of land.

Hill—an elevated, rounded point of land that is lower and smaller than a mountain. A **knob** is a small hill; a **knoll** is even smaller.

Iceberg—a large chunk of floating ice that has broken off, or calved, from a glacier. Icebergs often break apart into smaller pieces called **bergs, bitty bergs,** or **growlers.** About nine tenths of an iceberg floats beneath the water.

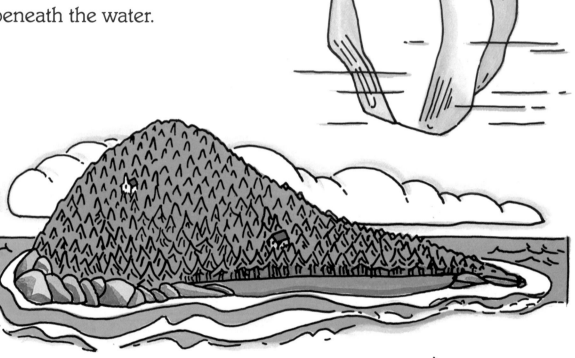

Island—a piece of land that is smaller than a continent and completely surrounded by water. Very small islands are called **isles** and **islets**.

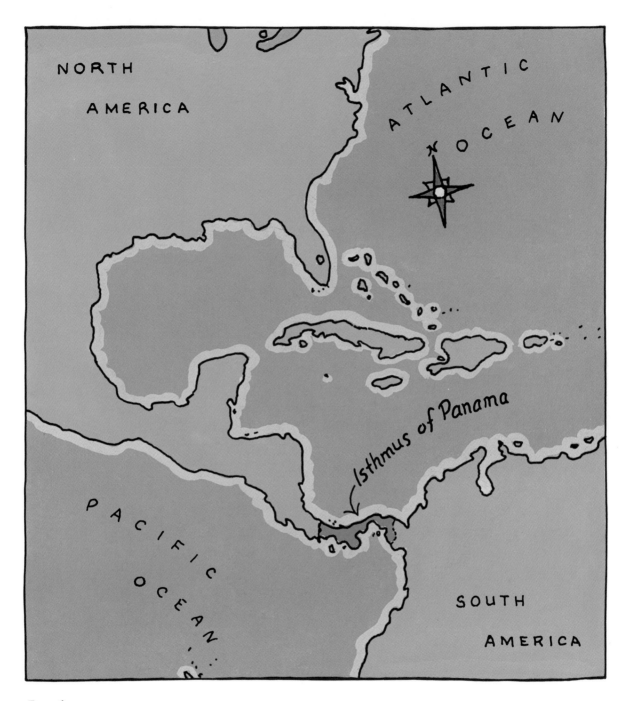

Isthmus—a narrow strip of land that does two things: (1) it connects two much larger areas of land, and (2) it narrowly separates two large bodies of water.

Jungle—a hot, humid, tropical rain forest. Most jungles are located near the equator.

Key—a very small, low, offshore island or reef. Keys are built from coral and sand.

Lake—a large inland body of water. Lakes are bigger than **ponds**, and ponds are bigger than **pools**.

Marsh—a low, spongy wetland covered with thick, healthy growths of tall grasses and reeds. A **bog** is a marsh filled with stagnant water and dead, decaying plants. Bogs are mostly found in northern climates.

Meander—a bend in the winding, looping course of many lowland rivers. Sometimes, the river channel will break through the narrow neck of a loop to create curved bits of water called **oxbow lakes**.

Mountain—a rugged, upthrust mass of rock that looms high above the surrounding land. Mountains are sometimes called **mounts**. Mountaintops have several names: **peaks, pinnacles, crests,** or **summits**.

Mountain Pass—an opening or **gap** in a mountain range that serves as a path or road across the mountains.

Mountain Range—a long, connected chain of mountains and hills.

Mouth—the place where a stream flows into a larger body of water. The mouth of a river is the end of that river.

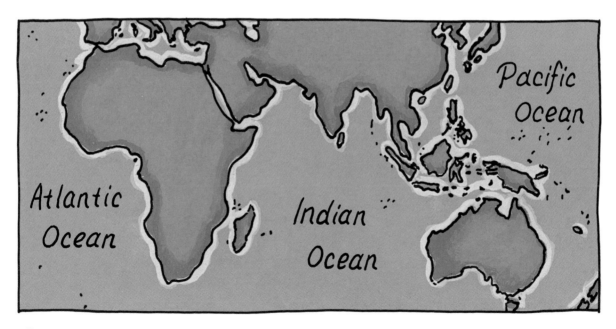

Ocean—(1) The entire body of salt water that covers nearly three-quarters of the earth's surface. (2) Any one of the five separate oceans: the Atlantic, Pacific, Indian, Arctic, or Antarctic.

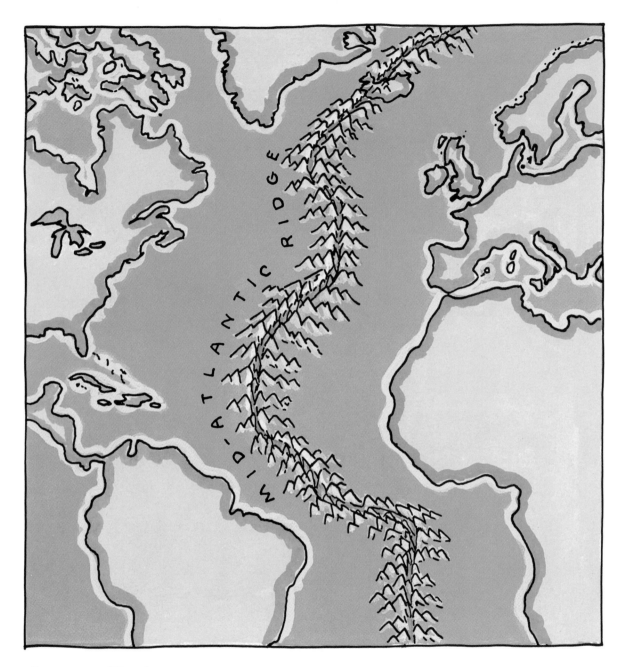

Ocean Ridge—a massive mountain range lying at the bottom of an ocean or sea. An **ocean trench** is a deep, narrow canyon in the ocean floor. There are more mountains and more canyons underwater than there are on dry land.

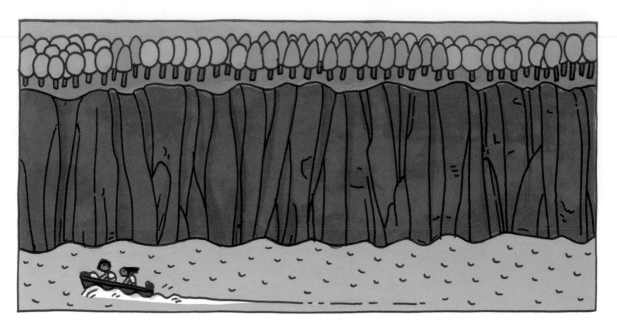

Palisade—a bold line of high, steep cliffs. A long palisade that joins two level areas of land is an **escarpment**.

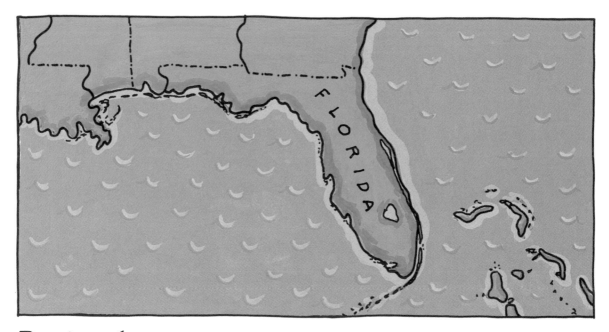

Peninsula—a large piece of land that juts far out into the water and is almost surrounded by water. Florida is a peninsula.

Plain—a broad region of flat or gently rolling, treeless land.

Plateau—a large highland plain that rises sharply above the surrounding land. Plateaus are also called **tablelands**.

Promontory or **Headland**—a high, prominent point on a rocky coastline. Promontories are ideal sites for lighthouses.

Rapids—a stretch of stream or river where the fast-moving current crashes against the rocks and boulders in its path. Seething, foaming rapids are sometimes called **white water**.

Reef—a narrow chain of rock, sand, or coral lurking just below or just above the water.

River—a long, large stream. Major rivers have many **tributary** streams and rivers flowing into them. The region drained by a great river and all its tributaries is called a **drainage basin** or **watershed**.

Sandbank or **Sandbar**—an underwater ridge of sand built up by tides and currents. Sandbanks and sandbars create areas of shallow water called **shoals**.

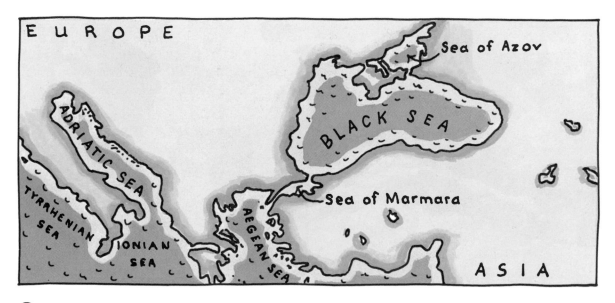

Sea—a large body of salt water that is smaller than an ocean. *Sea* and *ocean* are often used interchangeably to refer to great bodies of salt water.

Sea Cave—a hollow chamber eaten into a coastal cliff by the pounding power of crashing waves. **Sea arches** and **sea stacks** are also carved from these rocky cliffs.

Seamount—an underwater mountain. A tall seamount whose sharp, jagged peak is just below the surface of the ocean is a **pinnacle**. A seamount with a flat top is called a **guyot**.

Sound—a long, broad ocean inlet that is roughly parallel to the coast.

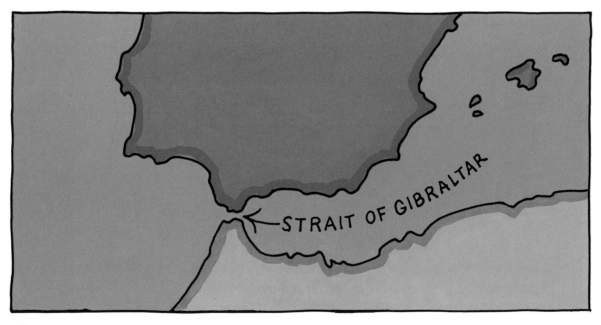

Strait—a narrow waterway that connects two larger bodies of water. Straits are also called **channels**, **passages**, and **narrows**.

Stream—a body of flowing water. A **brook** is a small stream, a **creek** is medium-sized, and a **river** is the largest of streams. The high sides along the edges of streams are called **banks**.

Swamp—a marsh with trees. Swamps usually contain more water and deeper water than marshes. Deep, dangerous pools of **quicksand** are sometimes found near swamps and marshes.